Dead Cen...

HAMNET

poem limited

a deadcentre text

OBERON BOOKS
LONDON

WWW.OBERONBOOKS.COM

First published in 2017 by Oberon Books Ltd
521 Caledonian Road, London N7 9RH
Tel: +44 (0) 20 7607 3637 / Fax: +44 (0) 20 7607 3629
e-mail: info@oberonbooks.com
www.oberonbooks.com

A catalogue record for this book is available from the British Library.

PB ISBN: 9781786822314
E ISBN: 9781786822321

Cover design by Jason Booher

Printed and bound by 4edge Limited.

Visit www.oberonbooks.com to read more about all our books and to buy them. You
will also find features, author interviews and news of any author events, and you can
sign up for e-newsletters so that you're always first to hear about our new releases.

Hamnet was first performed on 5 April 2017, at Schaubühne, Berlin, as part of FIND Festival. The cast was as follows:

HAMNET	Ollie West
HIS FATHER	Bush Moukarzel
Direction	Ben Kidd and Bush Moukarzel
Set Design	Andrew Clancy
Costume Design and Effects	Grace O'Hara
Lighting Design	Stephen Dodd
Sound Design	Kevin Gleeson
Video Design	Jose Miguel Jimenez
Dramaturgy	Michael West
Stage Manager	Barbara Hughes
Production Manager	Nic Ree
Producer	Rachel Murray and Matthew Smyth
Graphic Design	Jason Booher

Thanks to Annie, Michael, and Thomas, everyone at the Abbey, Willie White, everyone at Schaubuhne, and Jenny Hall

Hamnet was a co-production with the Abbey Theatre, Dublin as part of Dublin Theatre Festival. It was funded through an Arts Council Theatre Projects Award. Ongoing touring is generously supported by Culture Ireland.

Dead Centre was formed in 2012 in Dublin. They are Bush Moukarzel, Ben Kidd and producer Rachel Murray. Associate artists: Adam Welsh, Jason Booher and Ailbhe Wakefield-Drohan

To date, they have made five projects: *Souvenir* (2012), *(S)quark!* (2013), *LIPPY* (2014: winner, Irish Times Best Production, Fringe First, Herald Angel and OBIE), *Chekhov's First Play* (2015: winner, Irish Times Best Sound Design) and *Hamnet*.

www.deadcentre.org

@dead_centre

Characters

HAMNET

HIS FATHER

Nobody remembers Shakespeare's children

William Faulkner, to his daughter.

— What's your name, son?

— I'm Bart Simpson. Who the hell are you?

— I must say that in my day, we didn't speak that way to our elders

— Well this is my day, and we do, sir

The Simpsons, Season 2 Episode 4

Setting: a hellmouth.

The audience enter and see themselves – a live feed projected onto the back wall. They take a seat.

Eventually, out of the crowd we see a boy, **HAMNET***, stand up and walk on stage. He appears in the live projected image only, there is no one on stage. He stands centre, looking at himself.*

A moment of darkness and then lights up to find the real **HAMNET** *in exactly the same position looking at himself in the live projection.*

He's dressed in a t shirt, hoody, trainers, wearing a backpack.

HAMNET. Who's there?

Turning to face audience. Slowly approaches them, about to speak, about to tell his story but –

Sorry, I'm not allowed talk to strangers.

He puts down his backpack and takes out a ball.

My mother said I shouldn't talk to strangers because you never know who they might be, so don't talk to them. But I said to her, if I don't talk to strangers, I'll never meet my dad.

So… Hello.

Dad?

Are you there?

Maybe tomorrow.

Aims ball at the wall.

93 million, 2 hundred and ninety four thousand 6 hundred and 74

He throws the ball against the wall.

It doesn't go through.

93 million, 2 hundred and ninety four thousand 6 hundred and 75

He throws the ball against the wall.

It doesn't go through.

Not yet.

He puts the ball away.

I should introduce myself, but there's not much point, you haven't heard of me.

You'll think you have, at first. But then you'll realise you were thinking of someone else.

It happens every time.

I introduce myself and say my name and I see people's faces light up. But I know they've got me confused. They hear an "L" but really there's only an "N". One letter makes all the difference.

It's the same with my friend Andy: people get all excited because they hear "G-Andy". You see, there was a great man called Gandhi who changed the world. But my friend Andy. He's just Andy. He's okay. But he's no great man.

Neither am I.

Not yet.

But I've been rehearsing.

HAMNET *takes gets book from his bag.*

Learning to speak like a great man.

Learning the most famous speech in the world.

HAMNET *holds open book.*

To be, or not to be: that is the question.

I can't say the rest so I don't know the answer.

When I find out I'll be a great man and be able to do whatever I want.

Until then I have to do what I'm told.

Closes book.

I'm only 11.

But I've been 11 for years. I don't know why.

I only say 11 because that's what my mother told me but how can I really know?

Maybe she's lying to me, to keep me at home.

(Ask an audience member.) How old are you?

Audience member answers.

Who told you that? I mean, do you *feel* (e.g. 46)? Do you have any definite proof? You probably just believe what you're told, like me.

I was told that if you throw a ball against a wall infinity number of times, then, one time, it'll go through. It's called "quantum tunneling". Infinity means forever.

Gets ball from backpack.

So if I throw this ball against that wall forever, then, one time, it'll go through.

Aims ball at the wall.

93 million, 2 hundred and ninety four thousand 6 hundred and 76

He throws the ball against the wall.

It doesn't go through.

93 million, 2 hundred and ninety four thousand 6 hundred and 77

He throws the ball against the wall.

It doesn't go through.

I'm nearly at infinity.

He throws the ball against the wall.

It doesn't go through.

Maybe this time.

He throws the ball against the wall.

It doesn't go through.

Am I doing it right?

Let me google it.

HAMNET *gets his phone out of backpack and asks google.*

HAMNET. Google, how does quantum tunneling work?

GOOGLE. "Here's a summary from Wikipedia. Quantum tunneling through a barrier. The energy of the tunneled particle is the same but the probability amplitude is decreased. In quantum mechanics these particles can, with a very small probability, tunnel to the other side, thus crossing a barrier that it classically could not surmount."

HAMNET. I've no idea what that means.

Do you?

Pause.

If my dad was here he'd be able to explain it as he knows everything.

But he's not, so I use google.

He went away after I was born. I don't even really know what he looks like. I'm not actually sure if I've ever seen him. Except in my imagination, in my mind's eye.

If I saw him, I'd probably walk straight past him. *(Staring at same audience member.)* I could be staring him right in the face and I wouldn't even know.

Looks at a few audience members.

I guess he wouldn't recognise me either.

I haven't changed that much.

Actually, I haven't changed at all.

Turns to look at himself in the screen.

That's the problem.

I'm not getting any taller.

Sometimes I think I'm getting smaller.

I think one day I'm going to look in the mirror and see no one, nothing.

I don't want to be nothing.

I want to be Hamlet.

Maybe I'm too small for the part.

Pause.

Come on... grow!

HAMNET *waits for his reflection to grow.*

Nothing.

And my voice isn't breaking.

I'm trying to learn some Johnny Cash but it's hard when you sound like an angel.

Listen.

HAMNET *takes a small keyboard from his bag, sings the opening phrase of "Boy Named Sue" by Johnny Cash".*

His voice isn't low enough. Gives up.

See. No use. Voice won't break.

I sound like a girl. I sound like my twin sister.

I had a sister, but she's dead.

I miss her, but not that much because we've got the exact same voice. I hear her every time I open my mouth! It's like she's haunting me.

(In his own voice but strangely poised.) How are you brother? It's me! Are you being good? I bet you're not. Why can't I see you? Where are you?

(As himself.) Actually, I don't know where I am.

I'm stuck.

It's like I'm being punished.

But I haven't done anything wrong. I've done nothing!

You can't be guilty for doing nothing!

Literally, I've done nothing.

(To same audience member as before.) How about you?

You can't have been good for (e.g. 46) years! Surely you've done something if you're *that* old! Okay, maybe you've done nothing but you definitely look guilty.

Looking around audience.

In fact, you all look guilty.

HAMNET *remembers.*

"I've heard that guilty creatures sitting at a play have, by the very cunning of the scene, been struck so to the soul that presently they have proclaimed their malefactions."

What the hell is a "malefaction"?!

Gets phone out of backpack and asks google.

Google, what is a malefaction?

Phone answers.

GOOGLE. According to Merriam-Webster a malefaction is an evil deed; a crime.

Pause.

HAMNET. *(Into phone.)* Okay, google. What does this mean: "I've heard that guilty creatures sitting at a play have, by the very cunning of the scene, been struck so to the soul that presently they have proclaimed their malefactions."

GOOGLE. It means: when you're in a theatre you should confess your crimes.

Pause.

HAMNET. Does anyone want to confess a crime?

Pause.

HAMNET *feels guilty.*

Okay, I was lying when I said I've done nothing. I've done one thing. At school. I used a bad word.

Andy told it to me. I don't want to say it again. Something people do when they're alone.

He said my dad does it all the time.

I told Andy my dad would never do a bad word, he only does good words, he does loads of good words. And then I got all my dad's good words…

He holds copy of the Complete Works of Shakespeare.

… and I smashed Andy in the face with them. I think I broke his nose, I'm not sure, but there was a lot of blood.

I didn't understand Andy's bad word. And I don't understand these good words. It's just words, words, words. I'm worried that when I meet my dad I'm going to be left with no words at all.

That's why I've been rehearsing.

But it's hard to rehearse when you're on your own.

(To same audience member.) Will you be my dad?

Let's do *Hamlet*…

You play the father, I'll play the son.

Audience member goes on stage.

Stand here.

And say these lines.

HAMNET *arranges the stage.*

Stand anywhere as long as it's right there.

HAMNET *gives* **AUDIENCE MEMBER** *the book.*

Here are the words.

I'll just get your costume.

HAMNET *gets a sheet from his bag and covers audience member so they look like a ghost.*

Wait there.

I'm gonna get my costume.

HAMNET *goes to his bag and puts on some of his Elizabethan costume.*

You know the story, right? Course you do, you're (e.g. 46), I bet you've read it loads of times.

Basically, you're my dad, and you're dead – sorry about that – and you come to tell me how sad you are.

Okay. Ready? Go.

They read the scene.

GHOST. Mark me

HAMNET. I will

GHOST. My hour is almost come,
When I to sulphurous and tormenting flames
Must render up myself

HAMNET. Alas, poor ghost!

GHOST. Pity me not, but lend thy serious hearing
To what I shall unfold.

HAMNET. Hang on a second.

HAMNET *plays atmospheric music on his keyboard.*

HAMNET. Okay

GHOST. I am thy father's spirit,
Doom'd for a certain term to walk the night,
And for the day confined to fast in fires,
Till the foul crimes done in my days of nature
Are burnt and purged away. But that I am forbid
To tell the secrets of my prison-house,
I could a tale unfold whose lightest word
Would harrow up thy soul, freeze thy young blood,
Make thy two eyes, like stars, start from their spheres,
Thy knotted and combined locks to part
And each particular hair to stand on end,
Like quills upon the fretful porpentine:

But this eternal blazon must not be
To ears of flesh and blood.

Pause.

HAMNET. I didn't understand any of that.

I should've known you weren't the right casting. The ghost is supposed to be a great man.

HAMNET *takes the sheet off audience member.*

You don't look like a great man. You look like a nice man. But that's different from great.

HAMNET *takes book from audience member.*

Maybe we're not right for any of these parts.

I'm not sure what we do now.

Pause.

I know! Let's do the end of the play! It's easy. Everyone dies.

The key to playing dead is to not move. If you move, people can tell you're not really dead. Okay. Die!

They die.

Pause.

(From the floor.) You're really good at this.

We're great at doing nothing.

They lie still.

Try not to breathe too much. Be completely still. *(Whispers.)* The rest is silence.

They lie still.

What's your name?

They answer.

Nice to meet you.

Don't worry about the scene going badly.

At least we got the ending right.

I'm sorry I said you weren't great. I'm not great either.

You can go now.

Don't worry about me, I'm dead.

THE AUDIENCE MEMBER *gets up off the floor and returns to their seat.*

HAMNET. I'm dead.

HAMNET *then gets up, but his reflection doesn't.*

He turns and sees his body lying on the floor.

Okay, get up now.

I said get up.

I was pretending.

Don't you know what pretending is?

You're a terrible actor, I can see you breathing.

Get up.

The reflection gets up and joins him. **HAMNET** *is himself again.*

I choose to be.

I choose to be.

A figure walks on stage and is standing next to **HAMNET**.

We see **SHAKESPEARE** *but only in the filmed reflection.* **HAMNET** *looks at the empty air.*

Pause.

SHAKESPEARE. Don't you recognise me?

I suppose you haven't seen me in a long time.

Have you never seen a picture of me?

You've grown.

How's your mother?

Why don't you speak?

You look like you've seen a ghost.

Give your father a hug.

HAMNET *shakes his head.*

I've been watching. From the back. I didn't know it was going to be you. I got a free ticket so I thought I'd give it a chance.

You were doing great.

The song…

Especially the dying bit…

God, you look just like your sister.

Your face is her face.

It's spooky.

I know you're not sure about me.

I'm a stranger.

But you know it's okay to talk to strangers.

I mean, that's how I met your mother.

I wrote to you.

Did you see?

I'm still writing to you, in a way.

I'm not sure I have anything to say.

Just wanted to say hello.

I never say goodbye, it's a bad omen.

You play really well.

You sing well too.

A mellifluous voice.

HAMNET *shrugs.*

I'd really like to hug you.

Can we at least shake hands? As friends?

SHAKESPEARE *holds out his hand.*

Slowly, **HAMNET** *moves towards his father.*

HAMNET *raises his hand, is about to make contact but…*

HAMNET *vomits.*

HAMNET. What's a wanker?

SHAKESPEARE. What?

HAMNET. Is that what you're here to tell me?

SHAKESPEARE. No!

HAMNET. Don't you know?

SHAKESPEARE. No! Yes! No, of course I do.

HAMNET. But you said no –

SHAKESPEARE. No, you shouldn't use words like that.

HAMNET. Well, Andy said –

SHAKESPEARE. I don't care what Gandhi said –

HAMNET. – Andy said that's what people do when they're on their own and you went away to be on your own –

SHAKESPEARE. What are you talking about?

HAMNET. – to get away from me –

SHAKESPEARE. You're not making sense.

HAMNET. He said you're a wanker.

SHAKESPEARE. Stop it.

HAMNET. But don't worry I hit him in the face and if you look some of his blood is still on your book, see?

SHAKESPEARE *looks at the bloody book.*

Pause.

I see.

Pause.

Why don't you clean yourself up?

SHAKESPEARE *holds out a handkerchief (in the projection).* **HAMNET** *reaches for it. A handkerchief appears in his hand. He wipes at his vomit.*

Pause.

SHAKESPEARE. Is this what you imagined I'd look like?

HAMNET. Dunno.

SHAKESPEARE. Well, this is what I look like.

HAMNET. I thought you were supposed to be a great man.

SHAKESPEARE. I am.

HAMNET. You just look like a man.

SHAKESPEARE. You can be both.

HAMNET. Oh.

Pause.

SHAKESPEARE. I'll prove my greatness to you. Ask me anything.

HAMNET. Why did you go away?

Pause.

HAMNET. Don't you know?

SHAKESPEARE. I went away to work.

SHAKESPEARE *kicks the ball. It moves across the stage by itself and rolls towards* **HAMNET.** *He picks it up.*

I had to earn a living. It costs money to raise children.

HAMNET. How much do I cost?

SHAKESPEARE. Everything.

HAMNET. If I cost so much, why did you have me?

SHAKESPEARE. So you could meet me.

Pause.

I was joking. We wanted to meet you.

HAMNET. And was it worth it? Did you make lots of money?

SHAKESPEARE. I did.

HAMNET. What are you going to do with it?

SHAKESPEARE. I was going to leave it all to you. Turns out you were a bad investment.

HAMNET *looks confused.*

SHAKESPEARE. But it's all there. Waiting for you. The cupboards are full of food these days. The fridge is stuffed. The freezer is packed. For you. In case. You might want a midnight snack. Sometimes I wake up in the middle of the night and check. I get out of bed. I go to the cupboards and look, hoping they'll be empty. Hoping that you've come in the night, somehow, to eat your fill. But you haven't. The cupboards are always full.

Pause.

HAMNET. I got stuck.

SHAKESPEARE. What?

HAMNET *moves to book and sits down.*

HAMNET. To be or not to be. Which is it?

SHAKESPEARE. You have to make a choice. It's one or the other.

Pause.

HAMNET. To be, please!

SHAKESPEARE. Okay, usually it's not as easy as that –

HAMNET. Why would anyone choose not to be?

SHAKESPEARE. Well, because of… the "slings and arrows of outrageous fortune".

HAMNET. Okay

SHAKESPEARE. And the "sea of troubles".

HAMNET. Where's that?

SHAKESPEARE. You have to think about it.

HAMNET *goes to his bag to get his phone.*

SHAKESPEARE. What are you doing?

HAMNET. Googling it.

SHAKESPEARE. What?

HAMNET. Where the "sea of troubles" is…

SHAKESPEARE. You can't Google it. It's nowhere. It's a metaphor. What does it make you think about?

HAMNET. Erm… people drowning?

SHAKESPEARE. No. That's not really – why are you thinking about people drowning?

HAMNET. There was a picture of a boy washed up on the beach.

SHAKESPEARE. Where?

HAMNET. On my phone. On the news.

SHAKESPEARE. You shouldn't be watching the news at your age.

HAMNET. Did he choose "not to be?"

SHAKESPEARE. You shouldn't be watching the news.

HAMNET. What was his name?

SHAKESPEARE. I don't know.

Pause.

HAMNET. What it's like not to be?

SHAKESPEARE. I don't know.

HAMNET. You don't know much.

SHAKESPEARE. No traveler returns.

HAMNET. I bet it's boring.

SHAKESPEARE. They're two different places. Like different rooms. There's a room called "to be" and a room called "not to be". Once you're in "not to be" you can't go back.

HAMNET. But what if you walk through the wall?

SHAKESPEARE. What?

HAMNET. I've been trying to get this ball through the wall.

SHAKESPEARE. It's impossible.

HAMNET. It's called quantum tunneling.

Throws ball against the wall.

It doesn't go through.

SHAKESPEARE. It can't go through.

HAMNET. It's the idea that if I keep doing this for infinity then one day it'll go through.

SHAKESPEARE. No, nothing can go through there.

HAMNET. It can!

SHAKESPEARE. No, it can't. There is no infinity.

HAMNET. I bet it can!

SHAKESPEARE. Nothing goes on forever.

HAMNET. Watch!

Throws ball against the wall.

It doesn't go through.

SHAKESPEARE. I TOLD YOU IT CAN'T, nothing can go through there. Never, never, never, never, NEVER

HAMNET *is frightened.*

SHAKESPEARE. Sorry… I just don't want you thinking things that aren't true. I don't want you getting ideas in your head… the wrong ideas… I want you getting the *right* ideas… And it can't go through. I'll even google it.

SHAKESPEARE *gets out his phone and googles quantum tunneling.*

Oh… shit… it actually *can* go through. Weird.

SHAKESPEARE *reads.* **HAMNET** *smiles.*

Oh, okay. Hang on, you little shit. Look. Quantum particles are very small. But in the *macro* world – that's the big world, Hamnet – things don't work in the same way, even though the two worlds are related. You see, there's a problem when you try to understand big things by looking at small things. You get lost.

That's all I was saying. I don't want you to get lost.

Pause.

HAMNET. How many people die in your plays?

SHAKESPEARE. 74. I think. Ask google.

HAMNET *takes out his phones and asks google.*

HAMNET. Google, how many people die in the plays of William Shakespeare?

GOOGLE. Let me check on that… Okay, I found this on the web for 'How many people die in the plays of William Shakespeare.'

HAMNET *reads.*

HAMNET. Yes. 74. How many of those are children?

Pause.

SHAKESPEARE. Ask google.

HAMNET *asks the phone another question.*

HAMNET. Okay, google. How many children die in the plays of Shakespeare?

Phone says nothing.

How many children die in the plays of Shakespeare?

Phone says nothing.

Google…?

Phone says nothing

Bad reception.

HAMNET *puts phone away.*

Why have children in plays anyway? Aren't they unreliable?

SHAKESPEARE. They can be. But it's worth it. Children on stage are a sacrifice. Whether they die or not. Audiences love it.

HAMNET. *(Jumps up.)* Aaaaaaaah!

SHAKESPEARE. What's wrong?

HAMNET. I can't feel anything! My leg is dead! Pins and needles! Aaaah! Dead leg! Dead leg!

HAMNET *moves around frantically trying to walk off his dead leg.*

SHAKESPEARE. Stop moving. I'll massage it. Lie down.

HAMNET *limps over to his father and lies down.* **SHAKESPEARE** *massages his leg back to life.*

HAMNET. Dad?

SHAKESPEARE. Yes?

HAMNET. Who do you prefer: me, or Hamlet?

SHAKESPEARE. That's a stupid question.

HAMNET. Why?

SHAKESPEARE. Well, I mean you just – (*struggling*) there's no comparison, the two of you are so different. You, I mean, you're, obviously you're… And Ham*let* is from a totally different background. Very wealthy, private, intellectual. He's often very headstrong and cruel, lazy and self-obsessed, and he has a very complicated relationship with women, he thinks he can do anything. But I love him for his intelligence, and his commitment to honesty and justice, which is often overlooked in him, I think. He has a real conscience… *(Remembering his point.)* Whereas you… I mean, you're…

Pause.

HAMNET. What? What am I?

SHAKESPEARE. Well, you're… 11.

HAMNET. And a half.

SHAKESPEARE. What I mean is it's easy to know so much about a fictional character, because they're alive for such a long time. In fact, they outlive us. There's so much time to get to know them. Whereas people, especially children, like you… they're not as easy to know.

HAMNET. Why?

SHAKESPEARE. They're not around for so long.

HAMNET. Where do they go?

SHAKESPEARE. They're here one minute, then gone the next.

Pause.

HAMNET. Am *I* like Hamlet?

SHAKESPEARE. No one is like Hamlet. If people think they're like him, they're wrong.

HAMNET *is recovered.*

There. Is that better?

HAMNET *moves his leg. Tests it by walking around.*

HAMNET. See? Things can come back to life, can't they?

SHAKESPEARE. I suppose they can.

HAMNET *smiles*

HAMNET. I've got something to show you.

HAMNET *goes to his backpack*

SHAKESPEARE. What are you doing?

HAMNET. Getting ready.

SHAKESPEARE. What shall I do?

HAMNET. Wait.

SHAKESPEARE. What do I do while I wait?

HAMNET. A speech, *obviously.*

HAMNET *busies himself preparing costume and applying makeup to appear older.*

SHAKESPEARE. Okay. My first memory of you. Your mother's stomach was so big I thought it was going to explode. Of course, I'd no idea there were two of you in there. You could've warned us. Somehow. Kicked a Morse code against her belly, or pressed four hands against her skin. Given us a little wave. At least then I'd've known not to worry. I kept thinking, whatever's in there is going to kill her. She's going to die and it's my fault. I'd insisted on a boy. But it wasn't my fault. It was yours. You were born bad. And now there's something rotten in you. I know it because I feel the same rot in me. It's in my blood. It is my blood. I was going to come back, Hamnet. I was always coming back. It's you that went away. Forgive me. I'm living in the past. I haven't done anything wrong. I've done nothing! Really, I've done nothing. But that's the problem. You needed me. And I did nothing.

SHAKESPEARE *vomits. The vomit appears, by itself, on stage.*

HAMNET *in Elizabethan costume. Plays a flourish on his keyboard. He holds a child's skull.*

HAMNET. "Alas, poor Yorick! I knew him, Horatio: a fellow of infinite jest"

SHAKESPEARE. What are you doing?

HAMNET. I'm Hamlet, see?

SHAKESPEARE. *(Noticing skull.)* Where did you get that?

HAMNET. "To what base uses we may return…!"

SHAKESPEARE. Where did you get that?

HAMNET approaches the audience.

HAMNET. "They are coming to the play; I must be idle:
Get you a place."

SHAKESPEARE. Stop it.

HAMNET. "Get you a place."

SHAKESPEARE. I told you no one is Hamlet

HAMNET puts on a deep voice.

HAMNET. "Lady, shall I lie in your lap?"
Like that?

SHAKESPEARE. No.

HAMNET. "Lady, shall I lie in your lap?"

HAMNET become increasingly antic.

SHAKESPEARE. Stop messing around. For a moment. You need
to know –

HAMNET. "Do you think I meant country matters?" I know what
that means!

SHAKESPEARE. You're not Hamlet.

HAMNET. I know what "country matters" means!

SHAKESPEARE. You're nothing.

HAMNET. It means "grab them by the pussy"!

SHAKESPEARE. What?

HAMNET. That's what it means! I understand it, Dad!

SHAKESPEARE. Stop it!

HAMNET. I understand "country matters". I'm Hamlet!

SHAKESPEARE. No.

HAMNET. I'm Hamlet! I can do anything! I'm a great man! I can do anything!

SHAKESPEARE. Stop it, Hamnet!

HAMNET. *(With a flourish.)* GRAB THEM BY THE PUSSY!

SHAKESPEARE *slaps* **HAMNET.**

HAMNET *falls.*

SHAKESPEARE. Where did you learn to speak like that?

HAMNET. I don't know! I heard it somewhere!

SHAKESPEARE. That's bad language!

HAMNET. What's good language!?

HAMNET *starts to cry.*

What's good language?

Pause.

SHAKESPEARE. I'm sorry. I love you. Stand up. My son. My shadow. I'm sorry.

SHAKESPEARE holds HAMNET in his arms. In the projection they are connected, son in the arms of his father, but on stage, alone, HAMNET is leaning impossibly far forward, leaning in the air by himself for a moment, and then levels again, as his father rights him.

HAMNET. I deserve it.

SHAKESPEARE. No.

HAMNET. I deserve to be punished.

SHAKESPEARE. No.

HAMNET. There's something wrong with me, isn't there? I'll never be a great man.

SHAKESPEARE. You don't have to be anything.

HAMNET. I should go home now. My mum'll kill me.

SHAKESPEARE. Play me something.

HAMNET. I can't sing.

SHAKESPEARE. Me neither.

HAMNET moves to his keyboard. The backing track for "Boy Named Sue" by Johnny Cash plays. HAMNET sings.

Gradually, the sound of a full band and cheering crowd fade in. Father and son line dance.

SHAKESPEARE *sings the lyrics spoken by the father, then* HAMNET *again takes over, singing the words of the abandoned son.*

In a sudden moment, the sound of the full band and cheering crowd cut out and SHAKESPEARE *disappears.* HAMNET *dancing alone to the keyboard backing track. Just as suddenly, band and father return. The song continues.*

Towards the end, HAMNET'*s voice starts shifting off-key. It breaks, but in a strange, disturbing way, like a machine running out of power.*

HAMNET *finishes the song wishing to have been given a different name; not Sue, not George…*

HAMNET. Anything but Hamnet! I still hate that name!

HAMNET *notices his strange voice.*

HAMNET. My voice is breaking. I don't like it. Fix it, dad. Fix my voice.

SHAKESPEARE. I can't.

HAMNET. Fix it.

SHAKESPEARE. I'm sorry.

HAMNET. It's breaking. I don't like it.

SHAKESPEARE. I can't help you, Hamnet.

Pause.

HAMNET. Why did you come here?

SHAKESPEARE. To say goodbye.

HAMNET. That's a bad omen.

SHAKESPEARE. You have to stop haunting me, Hamnet.

HAMNET. But you're haunting me.

SHAKESPEARE. You have to let me rest.

HAMNET. You're haunting me!

SHAKESPEARE. You have to let me work. I've grieved long enough.

HAMNET. You're the ghost! You're the one who's not here. You've never been here!

HAMNET *walks through him. Stops. Looks back.*

SHAKESPEARE. I'm not haunting you, Hamnet. You're never going to grow up. That's the only thing you have to learn.

HAMNET. I didn't do anything! I didn't do anything!

SHAKESPEARE. You don't have to do anything.

HAMNET. I've done nothing! Aaaaaaaah! I can't feel anything! My everything is dead! Aaaahhh! Dead everything! Dead everything!

The ghost of SHAKESPEARE *stands centre.*

Blackout.

Suddenly, SHAKESPEARE *is there in person, and the real* HAMNET *is gone. Only the ghost of* HAMNET *remains. It is as if we are on the other side of the wall, in life.*

SHAKESPEARE. Grief fills the room up of my absent child,
Lies in his bed, walks up and down with me,
Puts on his pretty looks, repeats his words,
Remembers me of all his gracious parts,
Stuffs out his vacant garments with his form;
Then, have I reason to be fond of grief?
Fare you well:

I will not keep this form upon my head,
When there is such disorder in my wit.

SHAKESPEARE *removes his costume – beard, bodysuit.*

Forevermore, I am not myself.

Because you are gone, I no longer exist.

Your father is not your father.

I was only acting like your father.

It's a role I am not suited for.

The part does not exist.

You are alone.

The performer stands stripped of costume.

To be or…

Blackout.

Lights up. We see **HAMNET***, standing in the same place, the world as before, the world of not to be.*

HAMNET. …not to be

The performer playing **SHAKESPEARE** *watches. He appears in the projection only, dressed in the contemporary manner.*

HAMNET. Where did you come from?

SHAKESPEARE. Life.

HAMNET. Can I go with you?

SHAKESPEARE. It's no place for children.

Pause.

HAMNET. I had a sister, but she's alive.

Pause.

HAMNET *sees his father's costume on the floor. He picks it up and puts it away in his backpack.*

HAMNET. Will someone play me one day? Years from now? Some boy. I wonder what he'll look like. And who will play you?

SHAKESPEARE. It torments me to imagine.

HAMNET. And who will write me? Some grown up who's completely forgotten what it's like to be 11. They'll make me say things I'd never say.

SHAKESPEARE. Unless they're a good writer.

HAMNET. Did you write this?

SHAKESPEARE. I didn't write this.

HAMNET. Then who?

SHAKESPEARE. I promise you. Not me. I would never use you in this way.

HAMNET. Never?

SHAKESPEARE. Never. Never. Never. Never.

Pause.

SHAKESPEARE. Let us sit together until the moment comes.

Pause.

HAMNET. Dad, were you born before the internet?

SHAKESPEARE. Yes.

HAMNET. Dad, as a child, when you wanted to watch a film, tell me again what you had to do?

SHAKESPEARE. Well, we had to go all the way to the cinema on the exact day when it was on…

HAMNET. So funny. I love this story.

SHAKESPEARE. …and if we missed it, we had to wait until Christmas for it to be on the TV.

HAMNET. *(Laughing.)* Tell me about the TV Guide!

SHAKESPEARE. Yes, so the TV Guide was a sort of book that told you about all the films that were on over Christmas, and we all sat around and looked in the guide and planned our days so that we would be in front of the TV at the exact time when the film started.

HAMNET. The olden days are so interesting.

SHAKESPEARE *is gone.*

Dad?

Are you there?

Maybe tomorrow.

He throws the ball against the wall.

It doesn't go through.

He throws it again.

It goes through.

HAMNET. What a wounded name,
Things standing thus unknown, shall live behind me!
If thou didst ever hold me in thy heart
Absent thee from felicity a while,
And in this harsh world draw thy breath in pain
To tell my story.

Don't worry. It isn't very long.

I didn't do much.

I did nothing.

In this harsh world.

We did nothing.

HAMNET *walk towards the wall.*

He goes through.

The projected image shows the audience in their seats.

They all suddenly disappear.

The seats are empty.

END

WWW.OBERONBOOKS.COM